Alice Mead

Crossing the Starlight Bridge

Bradbury Press • New York

Maxwell Macmillan Canada   Toronto
Maxwell Macmillan International
New York   Oxford   Singapore   Sydney

For Arnold Neptune,
with thanks for his caring and support,
and for my helper, Erica

Bradbury Press
Macmillan Publishing Company
866 Third Avenue
New York, NY 10022

Maxwell Macmillan Canada, Inc.
1200 Eglinton Avenue East
Suite 200
Don Mills, Ontario M3C 3N1

Macmillan Publishing Company is part of the Maxwell
Communication Group of Companies.

First edition
Printed and bound in the United States of America
10 9 8 7 6 5 4 3 2 1
The text of this book is set in 13-point Primer.

Mead, Alice.
Crossing the Starlight Bridge / Alice Mead—1st ed.   p.   cm.
Summary: Nine-year-old Rayanne's life turns upside down when her father leaves and she has
to move off the Penobscot reservation and go to live with her grandmother.
ISBN 0-02-765950-X
1. Penobscot Indians—Juvenile fiction. [1. Penobscot Indians—Fiction. 2. Indians of North
America—Fiction. 3. Fathers and daughters—Fiction.] I. Title.
PZ7.M47887Cr 1994   [Fic]—dc20   93-40978

Contents

We are the stars which sing
We sing with our light
We are the birds of fire
We fly over the heavens
Our light is a star.

Passamaquoddy verse,
circa 1850

Chapter 1
Bronze

THAT SEPTEMBER, the year she was nine, Rayanne Sunipass walked to her grandmother's job every day after school. It was only two blocks from her school, and there were crossing guards everywhere, so it should have been perfectly easy to do. But those first few weeks, Rayanne felt her heart pounding nervously every time she entered the big high school doors and walked shyly into the principal's office. No one knew her here. She wasn't on the island anymore.

She always put her hand in her pocket and felt around for the crayon of the week. This week it was a bronze one. She always chose a special color, just to help herself out a little. Bronze was a color that was mysterious and magical. Holding the crayon gave her a special power that no one knew she had.

"Hi, Gram," she said, taking off her jacket.

Her grandmother was on the phone. She waved at Rayanne and smiled. Rayanne crawled under the lost-and-found table, her hiding place. Clothes were already heaped on it—forgotten windbreakers, sweatshirts, gym bags, and lonely sneakers. She was small for her age, and if she draped the sweatshirts carefully over the front of the table, she could read a book under there and no one would even see her. Rayanne was good at hiding.

Her grandmother was busy running off the school newsletter, and the phone kept ringing. She was the secretary for Springbrook High School, which had six hundred students. According to Gram, it was the busiest place in town.

They wouldn't get to go home until almost five o'clock. That was when Gram got done and cleaned off the top of her desk. Rayanne helped her do that. She put away all the paper clips and sharpened pencils for the next day.

Now Rayanne wedged her back against the wall under the table and started to read. She had to do a book report for school. Rayanne thought book reports were stupid. She hated sitting in class while kids stood up front, mumbling away about some dumb book that Rayanne had never read. To show the teacher how dumb she thought book reports were, Rayanne always chose easy books with big print and lots of pictures, books that wouldn't lead her anywhere she didn't want to go, books where nothing really happened.

Rayanne studied the first picture in her book carefully. It was of a donkey, standing on his hind legs and wearing overalls.

Let me guess, thought Rayanne. He's a farmer.

She checked the title. *Everett, the Runaway Donkey.* She flipped through the pages to make sure there were no dads in it. This book looked pretty safe. Dumb, but safe. Rayanne let out a sigh and started to read.

A pair of noisy shoes strode past the lost-and-found table. Rayanne knew a lot about shoes from the three weeks in her new hideout. These were black high heels with pointy toes. Shiny, I-mean-business shoes. They belonged to the principal, Mrs. Wilbur.

Mrs. Wilbur was Gram's boss. She was always in a hurry. Her shoes flew back and forth down the hall.

"Got that newsletter done, Hilda?" Mrs. Wilbur asked as she whisked into her office.

"Not yet," replied Gram.

"I need it by tomorrow," sang out Mrs. Wilbur. She said "tomorrow" like a song.

The loud clacking of her pointy high heels meant she was flying back through the office.

"I know you do, dear," Gram said.

Rayanne smiled to herself. That was a trick Gram had taught Rayanne—to say "dear." Gram said it kept people from getting angry with you. But whenever Gram said "dear," Rayanne pictured antlers stuck on the person's head like a real deer. It was a funny thought. But it would be even funnier if people said "moose," instead. "Yes, moose, I'll have it right away."

Mrs. Wilbur tore out of the office, calling out, "I'll be in a meeting in Room 321 until five o'clock."

That's all Mrs. Wilbur ever did, that Rayanne

could see. Go to meetings. Gram seemed used to it.

Two teachers came in, one with white shoes with navy blue bows on the toes and one with sneakers.

"Where's the Wilburforce?" the one with the bows on her toes asked Gram.

Rayanne heard the thud of the stapler. That meant Gram must be off the phone.

"She's at a meeting until five," Gram replied. *Thunk* went the stapler again.

Rayanne peeked out from under the table. The one who had spoken was Mrs. Madison. Her shoes were cute, but Rayanne wasn't sure if she liked her or not. She decided to climb out from under the table anyway. The Everett-the-donkey story wasn't very much fun to read after all.

Rayanne stood up.

"Hi," she said. Gram had told her to be nice to the teachers.

"These high school kids get younger every day," Mrs. Madison said, not looking at Rayanne but peering into her mailbox. She let out a hooting laugh at her own joke.

"Or else we're getting older by the minute,"

replied the short one with the sneakers.

Rayanne felt in her pocket for the crayon of the week and grabbed hold of it. She decided that she didn't like Mrs. Madison.

She squeezed the crayon and felt it grow hot in her hand.

The teachers were both laughing, but it wasn't a funny laugh, and Rayanne hoped they would leave quickly. The phone rang again and, as Gram answered it, the two teachers slowly left the office, leafing through their mail.

Rayanne went to the door and peered out in the hall after them. She heard Mrs. Madison say, "What does Hilda think this is? A day-care center? I can't believe the Wilburforce allows it, can you?"

"That girl's old enough to be home alone, if you ask me," the short one replied. "Didn't you say she was nine? She looks younger."

"Well, I heard there'd been some problems. The father left last spring. They lived over on Two Rivers Island. You know, the reservation and . . . "

They faded out of sight in the dim light of the late afternoon. The long corridor seemed to swallow them up. They disappeared.

Good, thought Rayanne.

She slipped into the hallway. Late-afternoon light shone in yellow patches on the floor. Rayanne stepped into one of the squares. Dust swirled silently around her in the yellow light. The floating dust reminded her of water. She remembered fishing at a lake with her dad when she was little, watching blue, jewel-like dragonflies dart across the water. The sun streaked its way into the shallow lake water, turning it a soft gold-yellow color like the light in the school hallway. Little waves had slapped at the sides of the canoe while her father fished. It was like being rocked in a sunny cradle, that's what she remembered.

She looked at her crayon. Bronze, she said to herself. Bronze. The sound of the word *bronze* made her think of huge, rocking bells or the swaying pond water she'd looked into so long ago.

He'll be back, she thought. Someday.

Chapter 2
Pink

EARLY LAST MARCH, near the end of an icy, gray winter, when Rayanne was still in third grade at the Two Rivers Elementary School, her father gave her a huge box of crayons for her ninth birthday. They still lived in their own house then, and Rayanne still had her brown-and-white rabbit. Her dad thought she should call her rabbit the traditional Abenaki word for rabbit, *Mahtekwehswo,* but Rayanne just called him Hop.

She got up early on her birthday morning to open her presents, but her mother stayed in bed.

"You go ahead, sweetie," her mother called through the door in a muffled voice.

"Mom, do you have the pillow over your head?" asked Rayanne through the closed door.

Her dad nudged her gently forward.

"She's fine, Ray. Working at the grocery store tires her out. It's a long drive from the island down to the Springbrook Mall. Come on. Let's open those presents."

Rayanne lingered at the top of the stairs. Something didn't seem right.

"Can Hop come inside and watch?" she asked.

"No. Last time he came in, he ate the cord off the lamp, remember?"

Rayanne nodded. Hop did make a mess in the house sometimes. She went downstairs and stared at the small row of gifts lined up on the living room sofa. She glanced back upstairs to see if her mother was coming yet. It was Sunday, a day Mom didn't have to go to work. She never stayed in bed late.

"Is Mom sick?" asked Rayanne.

"She's fine, Ray. I told you. She's just resting."

Rayanne reluctantly approached the sofa. It didn't seem right to open her presents with just her father there. Early as it was, he was already dressed in a plaid shirt, jeans, boots, even his tooled leather belt.

"Well, if Mom's not getting up, I'm going to go get Hop," she said.

Her dad sighed in aggravation as Rayanne ran to the back door. Hop's hutch was right out back by the trash cans. She flung open the door, and that's when she saw the red car in the driveway.

It wasn't their car, and there weren't any guests over this early in the morning, so whose car was it? Ray wondered. Everyone on the island must have noticed it parked there.

She slowly unlatched the cage and lifted Hop out. She held the warm, furry rabbit tightly to her chest and went back inside. The car was red and small, not at all like their big old van. It couldn't be theirs. It must be in the driveway by mistake, Rayanne decided.

She went back to the living room and sat on the sofa. Her dad was staring out the window. Ray didn't say anything about the car. She set Hop carefully on the floor at her feet.

"I guess I'll open my presents now," she said.

She tore the wrapping paper off the packages—new bedroom slippers, a stuffed panda, a little radio. Rayanne tried on the slippers. They were made of deerskin and were warm and snug on her feet.

Her dad sat across from her, smiling stiffly. Rayanne wanted to make him laugh, so she dangled the curly ribbons in front of Hop.

"Let's see if Hop likes to eat these," she said, but her dad didn't laugh.

She dropped the ribbons in a heap and started to open the last gift.

"Think you should go get the camera, Dad? Mom always takes pictures of this, you know. Every year."

He looked down and shrugged.

She tore off a little more wrapping paper. It looked like it was going to be one of those special big crayon sets. A deluxe one.

"Ray, I have something to tell you."

"You want Hop to go back out in his cage?" she guessed.

He shook his head and looked down at his clasped hands.

"Your mother and I need some time apart to think things over. I'm going to be going away for a while."

Ray felt like a big wind was blowing through her. Her body rocked a little bit as she tried to think.

"In that red car?" she asked slowly.

She forgot about the crayons and reached for Hop. Her dad nodded.

Maybe, she thought, maybe it was no big deal.

"Well, that's okay. When are you coming back?" she asked.

He lowered his head. Ray saw a little place on the top where the hair was streaked with gray like an old man's. She rarely saw the top of her dad's head. His hair was always so black, like a crow's wing.

Ray's chest felt tight. Hop scrabbled at her with his paws. She must have been squeezing him too hard. She set him gently on the floor. She was very careful with Hop.

Then her father began to speak.

"We should never have stayed here on the island. There's no work around here. No jobs. I thought we should stay here so that you would know how it was for me when I was young, but it's just not the same."

He stopped talking. Rayanne waited for him to say it was all a mistake, that he'd changed his mind about leaving.

Finally he said, "I'll call you, Ray, when I know more."

"Call me? On the phone?" she asked. No one ever called her on the phone except her friend Ann Marie.

He nodded, not looking at her.

"Open the present," he said. "I made sure I stayed for your birthday, Ray. No way I would miss that."

Rayanne held the gift in her lap with the wrapping paper a little torn. Nothing made sense. She looked up. Her dad smiled a polite, stiff smile, the kind he used at the bank or when he met her teacher at school. It wasn't right for birthdays.

Blankly, automatically, she ripped off the paper and dropped it on the floor. Why, she wondered, why?

"I tried to get you something special," he said.

Rayanne stared at her father. He used to look so big and strong, but now he looked small and unfamiliar, like a statue, like he was already gone and he'd left a statue that looked like him behind.

How could he be doing this to her? Giving her a box of crayons that she'd wanted so much and going away, ruining everything at the same time?

Her dad wouldn't do this. Not really. It wasn't possible. Maybe the two of them were cast in a spell. Maybe someone else, a witch, was making them do this. Rayanne decided to break the spell that held them.

As tears flew from her eyes, she stood up and hurled the crayon box against the wall. It made a loud thud, and crayons scattered everywhere.

"I hate crayons. They're for babies," she screamed.

Her dad stood up. He tried to hug her, but she pushed him away.

A few minutes later, he was gone.

Then Rayanne sat on the sofa and cried and cried. Her mother came down, and they cried together, until there weren't any more tears to come out. Rayanne's eyes felt swollen and her breath came in uneven little gasps. Her mother leaned back against the sofa.

"Guess we better pick up those crayons before we trip on them," she said.

Ray nodded and sat on the floor. Hop climbed into her lap. She slowly put them all into the box, their fresh, pointed tops like towers. She read the labels—pewter gray, cornflower, bronze, pine green, midnight blue.

Ray didn't think there'd be a tomorrow, but her mother kept talking about it. That night, Ray put the crayon set on her dresser. After she put on her pyjamas and climbed under the covers, her mother came in and sat on the edge of the bed. She rubbed Ray's back, but even her gentle touch seemed hollow and useless.

"Tomorrow, we'll have your favorite supper, okay?"

Rayanne didn't care. What difference did it make?

"Why?" she asked.

"Spaghetti. Or how about fry bread. With lots of butter?"

"No. Why did he leave?"

Her mom was quiet.

Then she said, "Remember when Dad lost his job last year at the paper mill, right before I started work at the store? For a while, he looked for work. But, then, I don't know. I guess he just sort of gave up."

Rayanne nodded. She remembered coming home from school, seeing Dad sitting on the couch, just staring out the window with the TV on really loud. He didn't seem to be paying attention to much of anything. Sometimes he went out, and Rayanne would be home alone when her mother got home from work. She wondered where he went. The Laundromat, or maybe the Community Hall, or maybe he just walked up the path to the north side of the island where the wild ducks nested and the river current pushed at the rocks. Sometimes he didn't come home until morning.

But that had been going on so long that Rayanne had gotten used to it. And some afternoons, she didn't go home either. She went over to Ann Marie's house.

"I guess this wasn't what he wanted anymore," her mom said, her voice tight. She took a Kleenex from her pocket and wiped her eyes and sighed.

Rayanne waited for a minute.

"Where did he go?" she asked.

"He's going to travel for a while, out west to Wyoming or Montana," her mother said. "Maybe we can wait this out, Ray. Let's try to be patient. Who knows? Maybe he'll come back. But you've got to understand, for us to get by, I've got to work real hard at my job."

Rayanne nodded. That had been going on for a while, too.

She thought of the photograph of Wyoming in her social studies book. Grasslands, prairies, far-off mountains. Tall yellow grass mile after mile. Maine was different, full of ponds and pine trees and rocks, like around Two Rivers Island. Penobscot, the rocky place, where the river swirls past our islands. What would he do out there without us? she wondered.

It felt to Rayanne like someone had taken a huge boulder and dropped it on their little house, tearing through the roof, crushing the floors, ripping the walls. And now they just had to live like that. In the ripped-up house with the rain blowing in whenever it wanted to.

Rayanne lay back and shut her eyes, exhausted. In her imagination, she saw the bridge from Two Rivers Island to Binghamton. From there, the road led to Springbrook and eventually up to Bangor. At night, the bridge stretched across the black waters, a row of lights twinkling in the darkness. The Starlight Bridge, she had always called it.

She saw the red car cross the bridge, its head-lights pointing west, far away. Finally the car was just two little red taillights, vanishing into blackness.

But Two Rivers Island was where they'd always lived, the Penobscot people, the people of the Dawn. She vowed she would never leave.

Chapter 3
Red

IN THE MORNING, Rayanne opened the crayon box and put a red crayon in her pocket. Then she went to school and her mother went back to work at the grocery store.

As Rayanne walked over to Ann Marie's house, she put her feet down carefully along the edge of the road. She hadn't told Ann Marie what had happened yet. Her mother said she would talk to Ann Marie's parents for her. But that didn't help for right now. Rayanne kept looking at her feet, hoping they wouldn't slip or twist in the cracked, chipped blacktop. The edge of the road was lined with icy old snowbanks, hard as rocks now, they'd been frozen over for so long. All around, bushes and trees pressed in, right up to the edge of the road. Just beyond the trees, the river flowed under the broken slabs of ice. Fast-moving ripples of river water showed through in jagged gray patches. The island looked different today, smaller and closed in. Worn-out, with old snow just about ready to melt to slush.

She felt like she might break. She felt like a fragile shell, with skin made of see-through plastic, like those models of the human body they sold in the toy store.

She thought maybe the other kids might be able to see through her, and see all the shocked pain that she held carefully inside. It was like carrying a cup of hot, scalding tea, trying not to bump it, so it wouldn't spill all over on the ground in front of everyone.

Ann Marie ran down her driveway to join Rayanne. Behind them, two fifth-grade boys ran until they caught up with the girls. The other kids didn't seem to notice anything different at all about her. Not even Ann Marie.

A black-and-white dog joined them for a moment, wildly sniffing the ground. Everyone argued about where it had come from. No one recognized it, and nobody mentioned the red car that had been in Rayanne's driveway. So far, her secret was safe.

"Monday again," Ann Marie said, smiling at her. Her voice was purposely bored and droopy, but her dark eyes sparkled at her friend.

Rayanne gave her a thin smile and shifted her book bag to her other shoulder. They always waited in Ann Marie's driveway for a moment. Sometimes Ann Marie's mother came out and gave them home-made donuts. Rayanne hoped she wouldn't today; she didn't think she could swallow one.

The boys started shoving each other. Jason pulled Adam's book bag off his shoulder, then ran off.

"Here we go again," said Ann Marie. Her mother hadn't appeared with the donuts, so they slowly started the walk to school.

Jason ran down the street a little way, then turned and yelled taunts and insults at Adam.

"They are so gross," said Ann Marie in disgust.

Ray nodded.

"I can't believe I have to let them stand in my driveway every day," she said. "My mom keeps telling me to try to make friends with them."

Ann Marie and Rayanne moved up on a low snowbank as the two boys started to tussle and shove. The girls walked carefully along the top of the crusty ice. Usually Rayanne was able to ignore the boys, but today she felt like screaming at them. Adam shoved Jason down hard on the ice, then dropped his book bag in the road and ran to get away.

Now Jason was chasing Adam up the street. Calmly, Rayanne took the red crayon out of her pocket and opened Adam's book bag. With the crayon, she scribbled red marks all over his homework. Quickly she zipped the bag closed again and stood up.

"What did you do that for?" Ann Marie asked in surprise.

"I can't stand those guys."

"Me either," replied Ann Marie.

The Two Rivers Elementary School was small but new. There were two hundred families on the island, but a lot of the island people were elderly. During the past year, some families had moved away when the paper mill laid people off, leaving behind empty houses with plywood nailed over the windows, houses with their eyes shut. Sometimes kids threw rocks at the boarded-up windows after school.

There were only forty-five students at the school now. Jason, Adam, Rayanne, and Ann Marie were all in the same class for third, fourth, and fifth graders.

Rayanne drifted through school that day. Most of the work she had to do was fill-in-the-blanks anyway, and somehow she managed to get it all done.

After lunch, her class went to the library to pick out reading books. Usually library time was Rayanne's favorite time of the week. The library had long, colorful banners decorated with Penobscot designs and a display case filled with beautiful handmade ash splint baskets.

A librarian visited the island once a week. Rayanne asked her if she had a book of maps of the United States. The librarian gave her a big green atlas with gold letters on the cover.

Rayanne sat down with it at a round table, flipping pages until she found Montana. She stared at the highways and the names of the towns. Helena, that was a big city. Maybe her dad would go there first, then head out for the mountains and grasslands.

Suddenly, her teacher was saying loudly, "Everyone should have picked out a book by now. Hurry and line up. The next class will be here any minute."

Rayanne shut the heavy book quickly and hurried over to the checkout desk. She pushed the atlas across the desk and opened the back cover so the librarian could stamp it for her.

"I'm sorry, Rayanne. Atlases don't leave this room for any reason. You can come in and use it here, if you want to. For now, you'll have to put it back on the shelf," said the librarian.

Blushing hotly, Rayanne put the atlas away. She had wanted to take it home. She hurried to the end of the line.

"Didn't you pick out a reading book, Rayanne? You had nearly fifteen minutes to find something," her teacher asked.

"Sure I did," said Rayanne, picking up a book that was on a chair.

"Let me see that."

Rayanne held it up. It was *One Fish, Two Fish* by

Dr. Seuss. The teacher frowned in annoyance. The children all laughed.

"I like the pictures," said Rayanne defiantly.

"You may like the pictures," replied her teacher, "but I certainly cannot count that as a reading book for a strong third-grade reader like you."

The class was quiet now, eyes on the floor, knowing a full-blown lecture on responsibility was a hair's breadth away. No one moved.

"Thank Mrs. Atwood as we leave," ordered their teacher, letting the moment pass.

"Thank you, Mrs. Atwood," the class chorused in a singsongy voice.

Rayanne said nothing. She was thinking about Montana and Wyoming. They were so far away. Her dad would need a horse to ride through the tall grass. Maybe he'd work as a cowboy for a while.

During silent reading, Rayanne looked at the Dr. Seuss book. She used to like Dr. Seuss books, but today the furry, blobby characters made her angry. She took the red crayon out of her pocket and made deep red marks on several of the pages. Then she shoved the book inside her desk and pushed it way back and pulled crumpled papers over it.

She raised her hand for permission to go to the bathroom.

"You may go, Rayanne. Are you feeling all right?" her teacher asked.

"I'm fine," replied Rayanne.

Ann Marie glanced at her as she squeezed by on her way out of the room. Ann Marie's friendly grin was more than Rayanne could bear. She started to cry as she hurried down the hall.

In the girls' room, she leaned her head against the cool pink tiles on the wall. She put her hand in her pocket and squeezed the red crayon until it broke in two.

After that first day, she left the crayons home for a while. Her mother had called Ann Marie's family, and Rayanne spent a lot of time over there in the afternoons until her mother got home from work. Ann Marie's mother didn't work.

They played games and dolls and watched TV like they always had, but sometimes Rayanne just wanted to draw by herself for a while. Then Ann Marie would sit at the table and watch her. Rayanne drew mostly magical things like toadstools, elves, sorcerers, and dragons. But it wasn't as satisfying to draw with someone watching over your shoulder. It was better to do it alone.

Once she talked Ann Marie into going through the fields and then the woods to the north edge of the island. Big blocks of chunky ice were pushed up there, the slabs tilting at crazy angles, driven up against the rocks by the river current. It seemed to Rayanne that the river water pushed so hard that the island might break loose and be swept away down stream. No noise but the March wind rushed in their ears.

"It's cold. Let's go home," Ann Marie said, turning her back on the wind and shivering.

And it was cold. The damp wind off the river seemed to blow right through their jackets. But Rayanne loved to face into the wind and let it blow through her, no matter how cold it was. She felt like the wind washed her clean, a wind bath, clean of school and math papers, dishes and muddy roads and worn-out boots. If she was lucky, the awful waiting feeling she had in her stomach blew away, too.

One day at the end of March, the girls stood on the rocks near an inlet. They heard the wild *con-*

coree of a redwing blackbird, and Rayanne suddenly felt happy for the first time in weeks. The return of the redwing blackbird meant that spring would be coming.

They walked slowly down the road to Ann Marie's house, stepping carefully through each puddle.

"Want to watch TV when we get back?" Ann Marie asked.

"I don't know."

"Want to play cards?" she asked.

Rayanne shrugged. "Maybe."

"You don't know anything," Ann Marie shouted. "Since your dad left, you're no fun to play with at all."

Rayanne fell silent. She knew she was no fun. It was because she was so busy waiting. Her head was filled with the waiting stories she told herself.

Maybe her dad was lost in the mountains or caught in a forest fire. She'd read that they had big forest fires in Montana.

Or maybe he was on a secret mission for the army, a top-secret mission, and he wasn't allowed to tell anybody a word about it. Not even Rayanne. And he wasn't allowed to make phone calls.

Or maybe he'd been out riding his horse across the prairie and a blizzard came up unexpectedly and . . .

Those were the stories Rayanne liked to tell herself when she drew the magic pictures. But they were private stories, and it was hard to think about them with Ann Marie and her mother watching her across the kitchen table.

One afternoon, as she walked home from Ann Marie's, she noticed that her mother had come home early. The van was parked in the driveway. Rayanne had never noticed how big it was. From where she stood, it blocked her view of the back door and the whole side of the house. Or maybe the van wasn't so big; maybe the house was that small. She hurried down the street and up the driveway.

When she got to the back door, her mother opened it. A newspaper was spread open on the table, but her mother quickly shut it.

"Sit down, Rayanne."

Instantly Rayanne felt the bottom of her stomach drop like an elevator that went down too fast. She glanced around the kitchen for clues, but everything looked the same—the cat's-face clock with eyes that twitched back and forth when it ticked, the braided rug Gram had made, the yellow checkered curtains to make things look sunny during the long, cold Maine winters, the flowered vinyl tablecloth with the tear in the edge where she had cut it with scissors, the sweet-grass basket she had made at school in her traditional-crafts class. Her mother had filled it with dried flowers.

"What?" Rayanne asked impatiently. "Just tell me."

She hated it when her mother tried to avoid telling her things that were unpleasant. She just wanted to know.

"I'm selling some of the furniture from the living room. The people are coming to pick it up tonight. We need the money, Rayanne. I'm sorry. We're almost out of heating oil for the furnace. We've got to stay warm."

Rayanne stared straight ahead. Her throat felt squeezed tight.

"Did you sell my bed?" she whispered.

"No, sweetie, of course not. Just the sofa, chair,

and rug. Oh, and the hall mirror. I figured we could do without that with no problem."

Rayanne nodded. Tears trickled down her cheeks.

"Rayanne, look at me."

She raised her head. Her mother's gentle brown eyes looked at her closely.

"This is something we have to do. We have no choice."

"Where's Dad?"

"I don't know, Ray."

"Well, he'll be mad when he comes back and finds out you sold our stuff. He'll be mad at you."

Rayanne wanted to hurt her mother. She'd show her that she was still loyal to her father.

Her mother turned her head away for a minute. She rubbed her face with her hands and sighed.

"Well, Rayanne, maybe he'll be a little glad that we didn't freeze in here, that we were warm," she said.

A little later, the people came to pick up the furniture. Rayanne sat on the stairs and watched them roll up the rug and cart out the sofa. She carried out the mirror herself, and they called her a big, strong girl.

When they were gone, the room looked lonely and bare. Rayanne's footsteps echoed on the bare wood floor with a hollow sound. She could hear her mother crying in her bedroom upstairs, even though the door was closed.

Now, thought Rayanne, the house is disappearing. Now anything can happen.

And despite her fear and uncertainty, she felt a tiny but unmistakable spark of curiosity.

Then she stomped back and forth on the bare boards in the empty room where the rug had been. *Stomp, stomp, stomp* drummed her bare feet as she got used to the new sound. It reminded her of the drums in the circle dance. Softly she sang a verse of the warrior's song, lulling herself with the rhythm.

Outside the window, the snow was melting, the first warm evening of early April. The ice had nearly left the river. There had been a warm, thawing breeze that day, but still the nights would be cold. The path that led to the door of the house across the road was all muddy. Watery gray puddles sat in the road. Puddles are pieces of sky that fall down,

Rayanne told herself. When they dry up, they float back home to the sky. She stomped more softly now, feeling the thuds come up through her heels, up the bones in her legs.

Then she listened. Her mom had stopped crying. Rayanne went into the kitchen and got out the beans for dinner. She knew how to heat them.

Chapter 4
Brick Red

THE END OF THE SCHOOL YEAR came and went in a blur. That summer, Rayanne spent most of her time at Ann Marie's house, riding bikes. Rayanne hoped every day would be a sunny one so they could go out. She hated the long rainy days indoors, doing quiet things like watching TV. She didn't want to play with Ann Marie's dolls.

Rayanne had never once imagined that she and her mom would live anywhere else, but now their house was going to be one of the empty ones, too. When summer was over, the day before school started, they moved in with Gram. Her gram was her favorite person.

But still, Springbrook, where Gram lived, was like another country. Rayanne didn't feel at home unless she could smell the river, the water rushing over stones so that the smell of stones became part of the air. Then the stony river smell floated above the river, joining in the air with the caw of the redwing blackbirds and the rushing noise of moving water. So that it wasn't just the smell that she missed, it was everything.

Rayanne packed her clothes in a suitcase and some grocery bags. She put her crayons and stuffed toys in a carton from the ShopMore that used to hold cereal. She folded up her blankets and her pillow. Now her bedroom had that hollow, stomping sound. Rayanne carried her things to the front yard and left them on the steps so that Ann Marie's father could help load them into the van.

Gram's apartment building wouldn't allow any pets, not even rabbits, so they had to leave Hop with Ann Marie. If Rayanne had to leave Hop, that was the best place because Hop liked Ann Marie and was used to her and wouldn't feel lonely.

While her mom and Ann Marie's father loaded up the van, Rayanne ran down the street to Ann

Marie's house. She hurried around back to the rabbit hutch, now behind their garage. She put her nose up close to the wire mesh. Hop came over and sniffed. Rayanne put her finger through the wires and stroked his soft nose.

"Good-bye, Hop. Don't worry. I'll come back for you. I won't leave you. Or the island. You remember that. I'll come get you, I promise."

Ray patted him until he lost interest and began to nibble at the tube of his water bottle. Then she straightened up and walked slowly around to the front of the house. Ann Marie came down the front steps. The two friends looked at each other shyly. Rayanne wasn't sure what to say. She thought she was going to cry.

Suddenly, Ann Marie stuck her face right up close to Rayanne's. "Call me a lot, okay?" she said in a silly voice.

She looked so funny that Rayanne burst out laughing, relieved and grateful at the same time.

"Okay," replied Rayanne. "Be nice to Hop. He might be sad at first."

Ann Marie nodded. "I'll play with him every day."

Silently they walked the short distance to

Rayanne's house, where the van was parked out front.

"Well, bye," said Rayanne, feeling awkward again. She turned around and walked backward toward the van.

"Come on, Ray. Time to go," her mother called.

"All right," said Rayanne. She opened the passenger door and climbed in. She rolled down the window.

"Good-bye," she called one last time.

Ann Marie stood in the yard, waving, as they drove slowly down the street. Soon they were heading toward the bridge.

As they crossed the bridge over the Penobscot River, Rayanne turned around in her seat and looked back as the island got smaller and smaller in the back window. She was leaving everything behind now, she thought, everyone she knew, except Mom and Gram. From here, all she could see was a thick row of alder trees and bushes on the riverbank and the muddy edge of the river. A car behind them pulled up impatiently and then passed them, blaring its horn.

Rayanne frowned.

"Who's that?" she asked.

But her mother had turned on the radio. She'd rolled down the windows and she sang as she drove, the wind blowing through her hair.

"Are you happy, Mom?" asked Rayanne.

"I sure am. No more driving across this bridge every day. Once we move, I just have to roll out of bed and I'll just about be at work. I'll be home at night at five-fifteen instead of six o'clock. That'll be nice, won't it?"

Rayanne remembered then that her mother had made this trip every single day. She sighed and flopped back against the seat. It seemed like all her mother thought about was her job. She was determined to do well, and nothing was going to stop her. All she ever talked about was the new management program she was going to be in. She didn't even care about leaving the island, thought Rayanne angrily.

They crossed the bridge and pulled up at a stoplight. There were two gas stations at the intersection. Instead of the smell of river water, Rayanne caught a whiff of oily gasoline and exhaust fumes. A tanker truck roared through the green light in front of them, on its way to Springbrook. Car after car sped through the intersection, while they waited their turn. It was so crowded, thought Rayanne, so many people hurrying past, past signs and lights and stores. At night, the lights were too bright. They blocked out the stars.

The stoplight finally turned green, and they headed south toward Springbrook. A half hour later, they pulled the van up on the tree-lined side street in front of Gram's apartment building. They walked up the path to Gram's entryway. Rayanne felt closed in by the redbrick walls that rose up in a U shape on three sides. Four floors of glassy windows stared blankly down at her as she pushed Gram's buzzer.

Suddenly, there was Gram's smiling face at the door, and it flashed through Rayanne's mind that everything was going to be all right, Gram lived here.

"Oh, Gram," cried Rayanne. She flung her arms around her grandmother and held on tight.

But it was going to be crowded in Gram's small apartment. There was one bedroom, a living room, and a kitchen, that was all. Her mother would sleep in Gram's room and Rayanne would sleep in the living room on a daybed.

Rayanne unpacked her stuffed toys and lined them up on the bed. Then she pulled out her sketchpad and tried to figure out a place to put it. Finally, she shoved it under the bed, out of the way for the moment.

Her mother came into the room.

"Don't unpack everything now, Ray. We've got to go over to your new school and get you signed up. I told them we'd be in before noon."

Rayanne sank down on the bed and stared at the floor. She didn't want to go anywhere right now. She just wanted to stay at Gram's until she felt settled.

"You might even get to meet your new teacher," her mom added.

Rayanne stood up reluctantly and sighed.

"Okay. Let's go."

Everything at the new school was organized around teams. Rayanne had been assigned to the Sky Team, with Miss Pinkham as her fourth-grade teacher. Miss Pinkham came down to meet her at the office. Then she showed Rayanne around the Sky wing.

"Our theme for the school is ecology," explained Miss Pinkham. "Each part of the building represents part of our ecosystem. The fourth graders study the sky. The fifth graders are on the Land Team and the sixth graders are on Oceans."

Rayanne felt confused. Her other school hadn't been set up like that. Besides, Rayanne liked doing things by herself, not with groups.

"That's great," she said weakly, feeling overwhelmed. There had only been eight kids in her class on the island.

"It says in your records from your old school that you are quite an artist. Do you think you could draw a logo for the Sky Team?"

"Do you mean a design?" asked Rayanne. She froze inside, thinking now someone would mention her being Penobscot, but Miss Pinkham went right on about the teams.

"Yes. Something about the sky that our team can use to identify with."

"Sure, I guess so."

Rayanne heard her voice sounding pinched and small. She knew Miss Pinkham was trying to be nice, trying to make her feel like part of the group.

"Thank you for showing me around," she said.

Miss Pinkham put her arm around Rayanne and gave her a little squeeze.

"Tomorrow will be fun. I promise."

Chapter 5
White

As Rayanne lay in her unfamiliar bed that night, she thought about the next day, the first day of school. Even after her visit to her new teacher, she was still worried.

Her mother kept telling her she should be excited to be going to a new school, especially a big, modern one like Springbrook Central School. But Rayanne dreaded it. She was afraid of being the only Penobscot in her class. If only Ann Marie were there, too, they could have fun.

School hadn't gone too well for her after her dad left last spring. She couldn't concentrate and got stomachaches. She tried to get the visiting nurse to send her home, but she hadn't been allowed to go unless it was an emergency because her mom was at work. Only kids with mothers at home got to leave when they had stomachaches, which wasn't fair. And then the nurse would tell her to "try a little harder," and "see if she couldn't forget about it."

She turned over. The unfamiliar sheets felt stiff and scratchy on her bare legs. She knew Gram put starch in her laundry. Rayanne didn't know exactly what starch was. Starch. The word had an odd sound to it, like a galaxy that was pulling apart, everything starching out faster and faster, like an octopus spinning in circles, its wavy arms being flung out, scattering stardust in a fine, white spray over the pitch-black sky, the stars spreading away from one another. *Star* plus *stretch* equals *starch*, she told herself.

Rayanne squeezed her eyes shut tight, trying to push the idea into her mind so she wouldn't forget it. Tomorrow, she'd draw it in her sketchpad. It was an interesting idea and it was hers and no one else's. It could never be taken away from her, even if someone scribbled all over her drawing or even if she took her sketchpad to school and lost it by mistake.

Now, lying in bed with school starting the next morning, Rayanne wondered if the twirling octopus galaxy was what Miss Pinkham had in mind for a design. Probably she wanted a smiling sun face or a cute little rainbow with puffy clouds at each end, something from TV or the card shop at the mall.

Rayanne had overheard her mother tell Gram that at her old school, they wanted to send Rayanne to a special art class, but that her teacher wouldn't allow it because she had fallen behind in her regular work.

Rayanne wondered if Springbrook had special art classes like that. It might be a good idea if she went to one. Then she could store her drawings someplace. Right now they were still under the daybed.

Rayanne flipped back the blankets and climbed down on the floor. She leaned over and reached under the bed to see if her things were still there. She pulled out the crayon box and looked at the rows of colors. Then she picked out the white crayon, climbed back in bed, and placed it under her pillow.

She thought about tomorrow, after school was over. The plan was that at three o'clock Rayanne would walk from her school over to the high school two blocks away. Then when Gram was done with her work, they'd go home together.

Rayanne was nervous about going to the high school. It was a tall, old-fashioned building with two round towers at either end. Ivy grew around the large, arched front doorway. Ray thought it was almost like a castle, mysterious and full of secrets. The halls were echoey and spooky and full of floating dust.

Her new school looked like three brick shoe boxes stuck together. But it had one good thing—ramps indoors for wheelchairs where there once might have been steps. Rayanne liked the ramps much better. If you walked down them quickly, your hair blew back in the wind and you could pretend for a moment that you were outdoors.

"Still awake?" Her grandmother came into the

darkened living room. "The first day of school makes everybody nervous. Even me!"

"Really?" asked Rayanne.

"Oh, sure, even after all these years. Maybe I should tell you a bedtime story. That might calm us both down."

"Okay," said Rayanne, sliding over so Gram could sit on the edge of the bed.

"Well, let's see what I can come up with. I might be a little rusty."

"That's okay," said Rayanne.

"How about a story about nighttime? This is called 'The Snowball Moon.' Your mother used to like this one."

Once far to the north, the winter nights were long and cold and dark. They were so dark that the little woodland animals could barely gather enough food to survive the winter. No matter how fast they scurried about for nuts and seeds, the darkness came quickly. Finally, Squirrel decided that something must be done. First she visited the field mice.

"Oh, it's a terrible problem," said Father Mouse. "We have so many children to feed, and the winter nights are so dark."

"Don't worry," said Squirrel. "I will help you."

So Squirrel went to see Porcupine and asked him if he had trouble finding food during the long dark winter.

"Oh, yes," said Porcupine. "But it has always been this way. There is nothing to be done."

"I don't agree," said Squirrel. "There is always something to be done."

"It's best to leave things as they are," said Porcupine. With a shake of his quills, he waddled off through the snow.

So Squirrel decided to ask Owl. Owl rested by day and sailed through the woods at night, with eyes bigger than all the other animals'. Maybe Owl knew a way to bring light to the winter forest.

Squirrel climbed high in Owl's maple tree and waited for Owl to wake up.

"What is it, Squirrel?" asked Owl.

"We small woodland animals need to hunt by darkness as well as day. The northern winter nights are far too dark for us. It would only take a little light to help us see."

Owl hunched his feathery head into his shoulders to think. He thought all day long, while Squirrel shivered on the windy branch. Finally, he said in his owly, hooting voice, "I will talk to the Sky Father and see if he can bring the stars closer in the winter."

Happily, Squirrel twitched her tail and raced down the tree to her burrow. Several days later, Owl stopped at Squirrel's doorstep.

"Tell your small friends that the Sky Father will bring the stars closer. But first, he must clear all the clouds from the sky. Prepare for a terrible blizzard." And Owl flew off.

So the animals gathered all the nuts and berries and seeds they could. Then they huddled in a hollow log and watched the huge storm clouds gather overhead.

For three days, the Sky Father piled storm

clouds in the sky, stacking them in huge towers. The animals shivered below, waiting. On the third day, the storm broke. A blizzard howled through the woods. The animals were frightened, all except Squirrel.

When the storm died away, a huge snowdrift blocked the hollow log. The animals could see nothing but gray shadows. They were disappointed, thinking more hunger and darkness awaited them.

"Wait here," said Squirrel. "I will tunnel out and see if the stars are closer."

Squirrel scrabbled up and up. Finally, she reached the top and her head popped out. She gasped in surprise. The winter stars hung so low in the evening sky, it seemed she could almost touch them.

A large, antlered moose stepped forward and bowed his head.

"I have been sent to help you," he said. "If you little animals will gather all the snow you can and push it into a giant snowball, I will carry the snowball in my antlers across the highest mountain ridges, where it *will shed light on even the darkest winter nights."*

And so, with the help of the moose and the Sky Father, the little animals made the first moon. And, despite the cold, the animals are happy in the winter when the stars come close and the moon shines bright like snow in the sky.

Rayanne smiled. Her mother had come in to listen, too.

"That was a great story, Gram."

"Didn't you used to tell me that one a long time ago?" asked Ray's mother.

"I guess I did. Or something like it. I don't know. I make them up, from bits and pieces of things I remember," said Gram, laughing.

"Gram, did you live on the island when you were little?" Rayanne asked.

"Oh, sure," said Gram. "Long before the bridge. In winter, we laid a trail of sawdust across the ice so we could walk over. But your grampa and I moved here years ago."

Gram stood up and smoothed the covers.

"Time for you to settle down," said Rayanne's mother. "Good-night."

When she woke up the next morning, her mom was sitting on the bed, smoothing her hair.

"Did you sleep okay out here? I was a little worried about you," she said.

Rayanne felt scornful. She wanted to push her mother's hand away, but as she looked up at her mother's face, she saw lines between her eyebrows, worried lines, and deeper, diagonal lines running from the edge of her nose to the outside of her mouth. Her mom felt Ray's eyes on her face, and she smiled. Her smile made the creases even deeper.

Rayanne knelt up in bed. With both hands, she gently smoothed the creases at the sides of her mother's face, and for a minute, her mother looked young again.

"I'm fine, Mom," she said, clambering out of bed. "I like being at Gram's house." She didn't mention the nervous dread in the pit of her stomach about starting school.

But then she went right back to being the old

Rayanne who couldn't find her sneakers and spilled her orange juice on her new T-shirt, and who, when it was time to get in the van, ran back inside to get the crayon of the week, while Mom waited in the van, yelling, "Come on. You'll be late."

Rayanne chose sky blue in the hopes that things would go well.

Chapter 6
Sky Blue

ON THE PLAYGROUND at the Springbrook Central School, the morning bell rang. The students, with their new sneakers and brightly colored backpacks, hurried excitedly toward the doors.

Rayanne hung back as the kids surged around her, laughing and chattering. She kept her gaze on the ground and waited until most of them had hurried inside to find their new classrooms. Then Rayanne followed the long hall down to the fourth-grade wing, where Miss Pinkham's room was.

In the classroom, the other students were already hanging their bags on coat hooks and finding their desks and then rushing off to see where their friends' desks were.

Rayanne stood just inside the doorway. Her mouth was so dry, she couldn't swallow, let alone speak. Finally, Miss Pinkham saw her from across the room. She waved above the heads of the children clustered around her.

"Come on in, Rayanne. Find your desk."

Reluctantly, Rayanne walked down the first row of desks, looking for her name tag. The pressure in her throat was unbearable. Tears backed up in her eyes so that she saw everything through a watery blur.

There was her desk at the end of the row. She slipped quietly into her seat, stuffing her book bag underneath, not daring to go over and push her way through the group of kids still laughing and talking by the coat hooks. She stared straight ahead.

Miss Pinkham bent down next to her.

"Good to see you here, Rayanne," she said softly.

Rayanne tried to smile, but nothing happened. She didn't want the teacher to think that she didn't like her, but her lips wouldn't move.

"You can keep an eye on my turtle for me, okay? See him?"

Miss Pinkham pointed to a large tank of pond water against the wall just behind Rayanne's desk. Rayanne could see a snapping turtle's scaly legs pawing the water.

"Maybe you can help me think of a name for him."

Miss Pinkham gave Rayanne's shoulder a little squeeze and moved to the front of the room. Rayanne let out a deep sigh and wiped the tears from her eyes. Finally, school was starting.

"Everyone take your seat," called Miss Pinkham. "Let's begin."

During the familiar routines of collecting lunch money, taking attendance, and passing out books, Rayanne began to relax and look around the room.

Maybe going to the new school wasn't going to be too bad after all. Miss Pinkham made sure Rayanne understood exactly what was expected of her, and there was a computer in the back of the room. Miss Pinkham introduced her iguana and the snapping turtle, which ate raw hamburger. There was also a telescope you could sign out like a library book and take home to look at the stars. Miss Pinkham explained that she wanted kids to challenge themselves.

After that, the teacher passed out a word search for them to work on while she filled out some paperwork for the office that had to be done right away.

When the boy in front of Rayanne turned around to hand her the word search, he said, "Where did you come from?"

Rayanne froze inside. She didn't answer. What if she told him she came from the island? Would he make fun of her?

He knelt on the seat of his chair and turned around, facing her.

"Where'd you come from, I said."

He was a wiry, scruffy, brown-haired kid, wearing camouflage pants and a basketball T-shirt. Rayanne stared at him. Finally, she gave a half smile and shrugged.

"What? You don't know? Boy, that's dumb," he said loudly.

Several kids turned around to stare.

"Scott," said Miss Pinkham in a warning voice. "Time to settle down."

"I can't believe how dumb that is," he whispered, turning around again when Miss Pinkham wasn't looking.

Rayanne tried to ignore him. She stared at her paper, words about Maine floating crazily in front of her teary eyes. Blueberry, granite, Augusta, pond. Kennebec River. Penobscot River. Her river.

A sense of confusion washed over her. There was the answer she should have given him. Why had she just said nothing? It was shameful of her not to tell Scott her heritage. How could she have done that? Was she ashamed of the island?

She looked up at the clock above the blackboard. Only 9:20 in the morning. Maybe this day would never end, she thought. She looked down at the scrambled letters in the word search, looking for the Penobscot River. Finally she found it, written backward like a word in code.

After math, it was time for morning recess. The kids all rushed to their bags and pulled out apples, cookies, and granola bars. Rayanne didn't have a snack in her bag. At the island school, they hadn't brought snacks. She didn't know it was allowed here.

The kids hurried out to recess in groups of three or four. Rayanne followed along behind them.

Outside, she drifted slowly over to the swings and sat down, pushing herself back and forth by rocking her feet in the sand. The September sun felt warm on her hair and skin. Three big maple trees lined the path to the school yard, a few red leaves scattered among the green. The bricks of the school glowed a warm, dull red in the sun, like dried blood on a cut, she thought.

Suddenly, Scott was standing in front of her, flanked by two of his friends.

"That's her," he said. "So dumb, she doesn't know where she's from."

"I'm from Two Rivers Island," she flashed back. "On the Penobscot."

One of the kids elbowed Scott.

"Hey, that's where all those rich Indians live."

"Oh yeah," said Scott. "My dad said you Indians are lazy. That's why you had to go and take all that forestland from us Maine people. You can't earn your own money, so you had to go and take it from us."

Rayanne knew about the land case. She had learned it in school.

"That land rightfully belonged to the Penobscot people. We just got back what was ours."

The boys looked at one another and laughed.

"Whoa," one said. "Are you going to take that, Scott?"

"Yep," said Scott. "Rich and lazy."

"We are not," shouted Rayanne. "That's not true."

"Oh yeah? Then what does your dad do? Huh? What job does he have?" Scott asked.

Rayanne stared at them in disbelief. How could they possibly know about her dad being out of work? How could they?

Suddenly, she leaped off the swing and ran at Scott. All the fear and unhappiness and anger of the past few months surged up inside. Furiously, she lashed out at Scott and knocked him down. Then she pinned his arms and sat on his chest. She spit in his face.

"Take it back," she screamed. He twisted his face to the side.

"No," he said, writhing to get loose.

"Liar. Liar, liar, liar! Take it back. All of it."

She dug her knees into his arm muscles as he tried to roll over to get away. One of Scott's friends tried to pull her off, but Rayanne leaned over and sank her teeth into his arm. The boy screamed and pulled back.

Rayanne got up, panting, and let Scott go. The boys ran over to the far end of the playground. Her heart was pounding furiously and tears streamed down her face. She ran blindly over to the big maple tree and sat down, her back against the trunk, her head hunched down on her drawn-up knees.

Someone must have told Miss Pinkham about the fight. A few minutes later, Rayanne heard her teacher's voice.

"Rayanne? What's going on?"

"Nothing," mumbled Rayanne.

"Rayanne, I want you and Scott to come with me."

Miss Pinkham walked them over to the double doors.

"Now," she said. "I want to know what happened."

Neither Rayanne nor Scott said a word. If she told about how the three boys had teased her, they would torment her for the rest of the year. There was no way her teacher could help her. It was best to keep quiet, Rayanne decided.

"What's all this about?" Miss Pinkham asked again.

Rayanne wasn't used to not answering teachers. She stared uneasily at the ground. Let Scott do the explaining, she thought. He started it.

"Scott and Rayanne, there is absolutely no fighting on this playground or anywhere. Is that clear?"

They both nodded.

"And Scott, you had better plan right now on having a better year than you had last year. Now, both of you stand against the wall until recess is over."

Rayanne leaned back against the warm bricks. She felt tired and drained. All the anger was gone. Whatever Scott said to her now didn't matter. Someday soon, she'd be going back over the bridge to the island, and all this would be over. She felt in her pocket for the crayon of the week and pulled it out. The sky blue color looked pale and weak in the strong sunlight. She made a tiny crayon mark on the redbrick wall. It was almost invisible.

She tried to remember Gram's story from last night about the squirrel and the moon, but she couldn't. So instead, she remembered the island. The bricks pushing against her back reminded her of lying on the big boulder at the edge of the little frog pond. In the summer, she lay on her back on the rock. The clouds in the sky seemed to fall into the pond and the water mirrored the sky and trees back up, as though it were all one place.

Chapter 7
Midnight Blue

AFTER THE FIRST DAY, Scott pretty much ignored Rayanne, as though their fight had never happened. It wasn't long before Rayanne got used to the new routine and even remembered to bring a snack for the ten-thirty recess. But she hadn't gotten used to being alone all the time.

The other kids already knew one another well and joked around a lot in teasy, loud voices, so that Rayanne didn't know what to say to anybody.

The kids on the island had teased one another, but their voices were somehow softer, quieter. But at least, so far anyway, no one else had teased her about coming from Two Rivers Island. Maybe Scott hadn't told anybody. Or maybe it didn't matter. Still, Rayanne wondered, was she supposed to just forget her old life on the island? Was she supposed to make it disappear? No one said anything about where she came from, so Rayanne didn't either.

Most of the time, she just tried to keep up with her work, especially her math and reading. It was still hard to concentrate, but her stomach didn't hurt quite so often this fall. She hadn't gone to see the nurse once yet.

Living with Gram was more fun than she'd expected, for one thing. Every night, they played rummy and ate popcorn.

Gram loved to play cards. Her eyes sparkled with excitement. Every time she looked at her cards, she acted surprised.

"What! Not this old jack again. Why can't he learn to stay out of my life?" or "You girls are in for trouble now. Might as well fold your cards, ladies. I'm warning you."

Gram pursed her lips, frowned, whistled, shook

her head, and tapped her finger on the table. Mom made fresh popcorn, and Ray lost game after game because she hated to discard anything. But she didn't care, it was so much fun to watch Gram.

Friday nights, Gram's bridge group came over. Then Ray and her mother would go out to give Gram some privacy. Usually they went window-shopping at the mall because her mother enjoyed it. Anyway, there was nowhere else to go.

The mall made Rayanne feel sad and lonely in the back of her throat. She tagged along behind her mother, past the store windows filled with new, un-familiar things, rubbing her forehead against the smooth, cool glass while her mother checked the prices on shoes they would never own.

Then Rayanne would turn and look at the fake palm trees and the plastic bushes clustered by the benches in the center of the walkway and wish she could go home to the island and feel the wind in her face again. She missed familiar things, her old cat clock and the yellow curtains and Ann Marie and her rabbit. And her dad burning the toast nearly every morning in the oven. That was the way things had always been.

Now she was on some sort of moving escalator, where stairs popped up and disappeared, and nothing stayed the same. The mall was nothing but windows with clothes and shoes that came and went. It looked the same week after week, but it never really was.

One day in October, just before recess, Miss Pinkham asked Rayanne whether she had made the logo for the Sky Team yet.

"Not yet," said Ray. "I need Magic Markers, and we don't have any at home. I could stay in for recess and get it done real quick."

"You don't have to do that," said Miss Pinkham.

But Rayanne didn't mind staying in. She sat down and began to draw, first a circle. Then, inside it, she drew an eagle. Behind the soaring eagle, she made a midnight blue sky with white stars spreading out in curved arcs like bridges, like the close winter stars in Gram's snowball moon story. It took her the whole recess to make it, but it looked good when she got done.

The children gathered around her desk when they came inside.

"Miss Pinkham, look what Rayanne did. This is awesome," they called to their teacher.

"Why, Rayanne, you did a lovely job. You really are a wonderful artist."

Rayanne was smiling and blushing. It really hadn't been that hard for her to do, and she was surprised at how much everybody liked it. But nobody asked her what the eagle or the stars meant. The eagle was a powerful bird. A sun bird, full of power and vision. The eagle can see far over the land and fly as high as the sun. And the stars? They were the People. But nobody asked. Rayanne went to the window and looked out, the lonely feeling tight in her throat. Didn't anybody care?

Afterward, two girls, Katie and Crissy, came up to her desk. They were both shy and quiet, unlike the rest of the class. Katie stepped forward a little.

"Will you eat lunch with us?" she asked in a soft voice.

"Me? Sure!" Rayanne answered.

So, thought Rayanne, smiling to herself. Maybe the eagle has worked his magic.

Chapter 8

Gold

THAT AFTERNOON, Rayanne walked happily over to the high school. The red and gold maple leaves were falling and the sidewalk was cluttered with piles of leaves. Rayanne scuffed her sneakers through them. She loved fall. On the island, the reeds turned yellow gold and the geese flew south. The sound of the geese calling made her feel wild and restless. You couldn't hear the geese in Gram's apartment. But she was happy today anyway.

"Hi, Gram," she called as she entered the office.

She tossed her book bag on the lost-and-found table. Mrs. Wilbur came hurrying out of her office, scooping up manila folders from a pile on Gram's desk. She glanced in Rayanne's direction.

"That table full of old clothes is a mess," she said to Gram. "We've got to move that out of the office sometime."

Rayanne froze. She glanced worriedly at Gram, but Gram just winked at her, so she knew everything was okay.

"If anyone needs me, I'll be at the superinten- dent's office until after five."

"All right, dear," said Gram.

Rayanne waited until Mrs. Wilbur had gone, then she went to Gram's bottom drawer and pulled out a little fold-up chess set and a *Young Beginner's Guide to Chess* book. Both she and Gram were getting pretty tired of rummy.

"Now remember," said Gram, "if you figure any- thing out, you've got to teach me."

"Right," said Rayanne, squeezing under the clothing table.

She opened the chessboard and started to set out the pieces. Suddenly, a big face appeared, upside down, peering at her under the table. Long curly hair tumbled down, almost touching the floor.

"Hey! So there *is* a kid living under the lost-and-found table. Cool!"

The head popped up and a pair of tattered red canvas sneakers came into view. Rayanne reached out and quickly untied one of the laces, then pulled her hand in again.

"Aaaah," cried the voice in mock horror. "It attacked me. I'm mortally wounded. Oh. Oh. Ugh."

Rayanne giggled as the curly-haired person collapsed on the office floor in front of the table. He smiled at Rayanne.

"Hi. Hope I didn't scare you. My name is Zak."

Rayanne smiled back and shook her head.

"What have you got there? Chess? Incredible! The Under-the-Table-Dweller plays chess."

Suddenly, Gram's voice called out in warning.

"Zak, if I were you, I'd get up. . . ."

The rapid clacking of Mrs. Wilbur's shoes could be heard approaching.

"She must have forgotten something," said Gram.

"Uh-oh," Zak muttered.

He pushed himself to his feet.

"What were you doing push-ups in the office

for?" asked Mrs. Wilbur. "Behave yourself, Zak. You're one of those students who is teetering on the edge."

"Just looking for my sweatshirt, Mrs. Wilbur," replied Zak, pawing hastily through the pile of clothes.

He dropped a nasty-looking sock on the floor.

"Woops," said Zak. "Dropped it."

He bent down to pick it up.

"Climb out of there when you get a chance and meet me at the water fountain," he whispered to Rayanne.

Rayanne watched the red sneakers whirl around and disappear. A moment later, Mrs. Wilbur left, too. Rayanne packed up most of the chess set and crawled from under the table.

"Gram, I'm going down the hall to see Zak."

Gram was on the phone and nodded an answer. Rayanne ran down the hall. Zak was leaning against the wall, looking up at the ceiling as though it were blue sky, whistling softly. He was short, with a mop of curly hair. With the red sneakers and his goofy smile, he reminded Rayanne of a clown. He turned her way.

"Oh, there you are," he said. "Thought you'd never get here."

"I came right away," said Rayanne.

"It's a little dangerous under that table where you hang out. Mrs. Wilbur could sneak up on you at any moment and KAPOW! Hey, is Hilda really your grandmother?"

Rayanne nodded.

"Kids say she kidnapped you and keeps you locked up in the office at night."

Rayanne laughed. "My gram wouldn't do that. She's nice. I live with her."

"She is nice," agreed Zak. "A lot nicer than the Wilburforce. So if you haven't been kidnapped, what are you doing here?"

"I stay here after school while my mom's at work, and then I go home with Gram."

"You mean you sit in that office every day after school? Gross! That's terrible. You should refuse."

Rayanne stared at him.

"I can't do that. My mother has to work a lot of hours and she gets really tired. I have to stay here. No one's home at Gram's apartment building. My mom and I live with her."

"So why don't you go to your dad's after school?" Zak asked.

"He's . . . he's not here right now," Rayanne said quickly.

"And your mom doesn't want you to do the home-alone thing?"

"Right," said Rayanne.

"My dad moved out when I was in third grade. About your age."

"I'm in fourth," Rayanne said.

Zak walked back and forth in front of her, flapping his arms. "Still, you've got to find something to do! Don't just sit there. I do something. I joined the drama department. We're building the stage set for our next play. It's about King Arthur. You should come see it. Your grandmother always comes to our plays."

"I guess so," said Rayanne uncertainly.

"Come on, it's going to be great," urged Zak. He stood on his hands and walked around the hallway upside down.

Rayanne thought of what Mrs. Wilbur had said about Zak teetering on the edge. She laughed.

"Get out and do something," Zak continued breathlessly. "You can't sit under a table for the rest of your life. You'll turn into a mushroom. A toadstool. A fungus! Do you want to be a fungus?"

"Zak! Come on," a voice called up the stairway.

He jumped to his feet and shook his floppy curls into place like a dog.

"Well, I have to go. They're waiting for me to hitch up the drawbridge. See you at the play, all right? Tell Hilda she better be there," and he galloped down the stairs.

Rayanne wandered back to the office, thinking about Zak and being a fungus and King Arthur. She thought she'd heard of King Arthur, but she wasn't sure. To her surprise, Gram was already tidying up her desk and getting out her purse to go home, even though it was only four o'clock.

"Oh, there you are," Gram said. "I thought we'd leave a little early today. How about we stop and get you a costume for Halloween on the way home?"

"Sure! Just let me get my chess stuff."

Ray dived under the table and quickly shoved the little pieces into the box. She hadn't thought about

Halloween much this fall, and she didn't know what she wanted to be. Maybe something from King Arthur. Maybe a princess. That was it—a princess.

She and Gram left the office and walked down the hall.

"Zak said you always go to the school plays. Can we go to this one, Gram?"

"Of course we can."

Gram opened the door, and they went out into the parking lot.

"Zak is a good boy," said Gram. "I like him very much, although I must say when I first saw him, I didn't know what to think."

"Why not?" asked Ray.

"Oh, I don't know. All that wild curly hair, I suppose. I was brought up in a time when decent young men had a clean-cut appearance. I know that's not true anymore. But, still."

"I think his hair is funny," said Ray.

"It is funny," agreed Gram.

The October air felt cold but fresh after the closed-in, dusty school air Rayanne had breathed all day. She skipped ahead of Gram and tried to do a cartwheel. It ended up looking more like a sideways handstand. Together they got in the car.

"Gram, do you know the story of King Arthur?" Rayanne asked.

Gram nodded. "It's a good story. Lots of kings and queens and knights in armor fighting dragons. But it's a lot different from our stories. Our stories are about the earth and the animals and harmony."

Rayanne thought about this as they drove to a discount store in downtown Springbrook. Rayanne jumped out and put the quarter in the parking meter. There hadn't been any parking meters on the island, and Rayanne thought they were pretty funny. She thought it was like paying for a car baby-sitter while you were in the store.

Inside the store, the Halloween costumes were prominently displayed in the center aisles. Rayanne and Gram crossed through the jewelry section, then the watches and gloves and hats, to the costumes. Rayanne sorted quickly through the racks, looking for girls' costumes.

"Hey," she said indignantly. "There are only two kinds of costumes for girls, witches and princesses.

But look at all the boys' costumes! Oh, wait, here's what I want. Look at this pink dress. Aren't these gold sparkles neat?"

She pulled the princess mask gently off the hanger and looked at it carefully. The thin plastic mask had pink painted cheeks and tiny, pouting red lips. Blond wavy hair framed the face. Rayanne held it up to her own face.

"Gram, is there a mirror? I want to see what I look like."

Rayanne took the mask over to a mirror in the nearby hat department and held it up. The pink face of the mask stared back at her, expressionless and vacant, like a china doll's face or a Barbie. The stiff, artificial blond hair stood out harshly, covering her own dark hair.

Rayanne felt her damp breath back up inside the mask, a film of moisture coating her skin. She felt like she couldn't breathe very well, and the mask in the mirror began to scare her. It wasn't her, but who was it? Maybe she wouldn't go out for Halloween at all this year. She hated the crumply green skin of the witches' masks, but she could never be a princess, not this kind. Then who was she supposed to be?

She took the mask off and stood in front of the mirror, not moving. She felt her cheeks grow hot in her confusion. Who cares about a dumb old costume, she told herself. She hurried back to the rack and hung up the mask.

"I guess I really don't want to buy anything right now," she mumbled.

Gram looked at her curiously, but Rayanne kept her head down.

"Is all that pink stuff too flouncy for you?" asked Gram lightly.

Ray nodded. "Let's go, okay?"

Gram took her hand. Rayanne held on firmly as they left the store.

"Now, let's see," said Gram to herself as they got back in the car. "What could you be for Halloween? An owl or a bear, maybe, or are you too old for animals? Of course, I've always wanted to be a fortuneteller with a crystal ball."

"I know," Rayanne said, flinging herself back against the seat. "I could be a magician with a top

hat and a magic wand. The kind who can make rabbits come out of their hats."

Gram didn't say anything for a minute.

"What do you think, Gram? Do you think I could
be a magician?" Ray persisted.

"Sure. I bet we could find a top hat someplace."

As Rayanne leaned back, planning her costume,
Gram concentrated on her driving, and it was quiet
in the car the rest of the way home.

Chapter 9
Gray

THE NEXT DAY was Saturday. For once, Rayanne found herself missing school. She wondered what Katie and Crissy were doing. Maybe someday she could invite them over.

Not only was it Saturday, but it was raining a hard, cold rain that knocked the red and gold leaves off the trees and plastered them to the streets and sidewalks. The trees tossed wet and black in the wind.

Rayanne's mother had to go to work, and there were no other children in Gram's apartment building for Rayanne to play with. In rainy, windy weather on the island, Rayanne had liked to go down to the rain-swollen river and watch it rush by, pushing and swirling its way to the sea.

Now, for an hour, Rayanne got out her crayons and made drawings of castles and fair ladies and dragons. But then she got restless. Her drawings all looked like things she had drawn before. She wanted to draw something different. She tried to draw the moose carrying the moon in his antlers, but she drew him wrong. He looked like a big brown dog. She needed a picture to look at. She put her crayons down and went off to find Gram. She sat on the edge of the tub and watched Gram scrub the sink.

"Gram, who is Merlin?" she asked.

Gram handed Ray a sponge.

"He's a magician in the King Arthur story. Here, give me a hand, Ray, so we can get these chores over with. There's nothing I hate worse than cleaning bathrooms."

Rayanne scrubbed the tiles around the bathtub. Everything looked perfectly clean to her. She couldn't see any reason to make it look cleaner.

"And," said Gram, refilling the sink with clean

water, "he's a powerful magician. But then again, so is Koluskap."

Rayanne idly swiped the edge of the tub with the sponge. She had learned in her old school how Koluskap rose tall enough to touch the stars and how he made the first man and woman from the ash tree.

"Gram, can we go to the library later?" she asked.

Her grandmother paused while cleaning the mirror, and looked at her with raised eyebrows.

"The library? I thought we were going to have a go at chess."

"But we can play chess *and* go to the library. I need to get a book about a moose. I'm trying to draw a picture about that last story you told me. Then when Dad calls, I can send it to him," Rayanne said with satisfaction.

Gram put the sponge and spray cleaner down.

"Let's take a break," she said. "Let's go in the kitchen and have some tea."

"Tea? Okay," agreed Rayanne, surprised. She didn't usually drink tea.

Her grandmother boiled water and set out two mugs.

"You know, in the old way, I am your respected grandmother and teacher, right?" Gram asked.

Rayanne shrugged.

"I guess so," she said.

Gram poured the tea and handed her a cup.

"Careful, Ray. I don't want you to burn your tongue," said Gram.

"I won't. See? I'll blow on it and then just take a little sip."

Instantly, Rayanne scalded the tip of her tongue. She set the mug down quickly and didn't say a word. She caught Gram looking at her and knew she hadn't listened.

"Ray, I guess you miss your dad a lot. But I don't think he'll be coming around here anytime too soon. It's sad for me to watch this happen to such a good little girl like you."

A good girl? thought Rayanne, her heart warming at the praise.

"He didn't leave because I was bad? I wasn't very good about keeping Hop outside in his cage."

"What an idea!" exclaimed Gram.

"Well, then how come he hasn't called me yet? He said he would. I think it's probably because in

Montana, it's so far to town. There are probably no phone booths."

"Listen, Rayanne, I know your mother lets you think he's very far away. She has a hard time discussing this with you. But your dad left because he was feeling restless and confused. He doesn't call because he feels bad."

"He does?" asked Rayanne, startled. She stared at the hot tea. Well, then he must need my help, she thought. I'd better help him out.

"Maybe we should call him," she said.

"Maybe," said Gram carefully. "But he's not in Montana at all now. He's right here in Maine. One of the teachers at school saw him last weekend."

"But why didn't he find me? I don't believe you, Gram. You made that up. I bet it was that stupid Mrs. Madison that said that. I hate her."

She burst into tears. Gram led her gently to the sofa and sat down with her.

"I'm sorry, Ray. I know it doesn't help one bit, but I am sorry. Your mom and I are your family now."

"I just don't want anything else to happen. Why did Mom have to marry someone who would go away? She should have known better."

Gram held Ray and rocked her.

"Now, Ray, your mother never dreamed this would happen. You see, your mother is very patient and your father is kind of restless."

"Am I restless?"

"Yes, a little. But curious, too. And you wait patiently for me at work every day. You've never once complained."

Rayanne smiled.

"Anyway," continued Gram, "it's hard for us to live in two worlds at the same time. The world of TV and rich, white people that you see everywhere. Many people trying to buy happiness. But you were raised on the island. Your dad wanted you to know about your ancient heritage. Sometimes, surrounded by white culture, you feel you have nowhere to go, feeling apart from the rest. Kind of a homesick feeling."

Rayanne nodded. "Is homesickness that achy feeling in your throat?" She hadn't understood everything Gram had said, but she understood that part.

Gram nodded. "I think that's how your dad feels. He's not sure where to go right now."

"I like the island better," said Rayanne.

"Well, yes," said Gram. "But you have to be able to cross the bridge back and forth. Make new ways from the old. Koluskap said the stars are our brothers. You should remember that. And even before the white people came, Koluskap said every Penobscot has to think for himself, to find his own way. Like the magic rabbit, Mahtekwchswo. He made up his own way."

Rayanne smiled a little through her tears.

"And look at you," said Gram. "Off getting a book on King Arthur and learning chess and making new friends at school. Did I know my shy Rayanne would be doing all that last week? No, I did not."

Rayanne laughed and sniffed and laughed again.

"I guess I'm full of surprises," she said.

"I guess you are," answered Gram. "Let's stop cleaning bathrooms and go get your library book. Then maybe we can stop in and surprise your mother at the grocery store."

At the library, Rayanne took out a book on Maine animals as well as ones on King Arthur and life in medieval times. She and Gram hid the books under their coats as they darted through the rain to Gram's car. Rayanne ran around to her side and yanked the door open. She collapsed on the front seat. Her hair hung down in damp strings, and her sneakers were soaked.

"Whew," she exclaimed, wiping her face. "We should have brought an umbrella."

"Oh well," said Gram.

Rayanne started flipping through the King Arthur book as Gram drove past the park, heading out of town to the mall where the ShopMore was.

"Look at these clunky suits of armor. Don't you feel sorry for the horses? Those guys must have weighed a ton. Here's the dungeon and the torture chamber. At the feast, they ate roast sparrow pie with ale. That's disgusting. And a pig's head served on a platter! No, thanks. Where's the part about Merlin the magician?"

Rayanne fell silent as she studied the pictures. Soon she was reading the story of King Arthur. Gram drove through the heavy rain and pulled into the parking lot of the ShopMore.

"Okay, Ray. Out," said Gram, pulling up her collar and getting ready to jump out.

"We're here already?" Rayanne asked. She undid her seat belt and paused.

"Did we bring Mom a treat?" she asked. "I thought we were going to."

"I thought maybe we could take her out to lunch."

"Chinese food?" asked Rayanne excitedly.

"Does she like Chinese food?"

"Yes."

"Okay then."

Together, they darted into the store. There was Rayanne's mother up front by the big windows in her orange ShopMore blazer, smiling and walking back and forth, helping people as they needed it. She was training to be a manager.

Rayanne was surprised to see how different her mother looked at work. By the time she got home at night, she always looked so worn and tired. Managers worked a lot of hours. But here, she looked happy, solving problems for the customers. Everybody seemed to know her. Almost all the people carrying their groceries out called to her and smiled at her.

Her mother looked happier here than she sometimes did at home. Rayanne scowled and kicked jealously at the wheel of a shopping cart that blocked her way. Then she took the empty cart and shoved it into the row of pushed-together carts by the door. The cart rattled into place with a small, satisfying crash. Rayanne turned and looked at her grandmother.

"Your mother does a good job here, Ray. Run over and ask her when her lunch break is. And ask her about that Chinese food."

After dinner that night, they did the dishes together. As Gram dried her hands on the dish towel, she said, "All right, Rayanne. I'm ready for another story. But I'll have to tell it to you now, or I might forget it."

They went into the living room and sat together on the sofa, and Gram began.

"This is called 'The Clown of the Pond' and it's about how the loon, the messenger, got its laugh."

Just before sunrise, when ponds wake up, they ripple their surface and push the pearly gray mist into the reeds. Box Turtle blinked at the gray sunlight, then snuggled into his muddy nest. Silly Loon had kept him awake, with her fussing and flapping all night long. He scrabbled at the mud and tucked his head into his shell, feeling grumpy.

In the reeds, Wild Swan hid her beak in her snowy chest feathers. Loon had kept her awake, too, and just because she'd laid an egg. What silliness!

Then the sun shot rays of yellow light over the hill, piercing the gray mist. The sunlight startled Silly Loon. She was a nervous bird. Everything startled her, and now she had a new egg to take care of. She'd had a busy night.

As the sun warmed the surface of the pond, waking the insects, Loon left her nest and dived deep into the water. Far below in the black, cool water, she woke the sleeping fish, swimming and twisting and turning through the long water-lily stems. Then she popped up for air right by Turtle's mudbank.

Turtle was a gentle, patient creature and he tried to give Loon some advice. Perhaps she *had not been well taught by her elders.*

"Go to sleep. Find a warm, rotted branch in the sun, climb on it, eat a few bugs, and doze all day. Then you will have a long life like me."

Loon was startled by Turtle's speech. She stretched her big black wings wide and flapped backward in the water, sending rippling waves into Turtle's nest. She cast her beak east and west and dived deep into the pond. Waves washed into Turtle's nest.

Turtle carefully pushed new mud into the place where the washout had occurred and went back to sleep.

Meanwhile, Swan sailed across the pond. She saw Loon. Poor Loon, thought Swan, she looks so silly in those spotted feathers. She is the clown of the pond. I shall give her some advice. Swan glided smoothly up to Loon.

"Be calm at all times, like me," said the swan. "And hold your head high. Arch your neck. Be just like me."

Loon swam off to be by herself. Sleeping was not what she did best. And her neck did not stretch up high like Swan's. So what did she do best? If anything, Loon was watchful and alert. She noticed every little change at the pond.

She paddled around her little island where her nest was.

"I shall announce every little thing that I see, day or night. Then Swan and Turtle will see that I am important, too."

Loon paddled to her nest and looked at her egg. "See how round and brown my egg is! I shall announce it."

She stretched back her head and let out the wildest, silliest hooting song ever heard in the woods of Maine. "Hoo, hoo, hoo," she sang.

Late that night, as Loon stepped off her nest to turn her egg, she looked up and saw the stars pressing down from a black velvet sky.

"See how the stars shine like jewels. Hoo, hoo, hoo."

Her wild call echoed off the hills rimming the pond. It woke the children sleeping in the valley below. They looked out and saw the bright stars that Loon wanted them to see.

They fell back asleep, reassured that nothing had changed.

Gram folded her hands in her lap when she was done. Rayanne thought it was the best story she'd ever heard. Later, as she lay in bed, she thought about it.

What can I do? she wondered. I can take care of my rabbit. I made him a promise. Maybe I can find a way to get Hop back. I promised I would.

She fell asleep, thinking of a plan.

Chapter 10
Pine Green

MONDAY MORNING, Rayanne arrived at school both nervous and determined. This was the day she would try to convince Miss Pinkham to let Hop come to stay in their classroom. After all, they already had an iguana and a snapping turtle. Why not a rabbit?

Rayanne hurried in from the playground early and waited at the classroom door, hoping to catch Miss Pinkham before all the hundreds of details of the day took over.

Suddenly, there she was, hurrying down the hall with her canvas tote bag full of corrected papers.

Her brown, curly hair fluffed out around her face and her glasses were sliding down her nose.

"Miss Pinkham?" Rayanne stepped forward.

She stopped and pushed up her glasses.

"Why, yes, Rayanne. What is it? You're here early."

"I have to ask you something."

"Certainly."

Miss Pinkham stopped and gave Rayanne her full attention. She wasn't the friendliest teacher, the kids said, but she was fair and clear and gave each student her direct attention. Suddenly, Rayanne realized that maybe that was better than fuzzy friendliness.

With renewed confidence at being taken seriously, Rayanne said, "I wondered if it would be all right, if you wouldn't mind, that is . . . "

Miss Pinkham smiled broadly.

"Go ahead and ask me, Rayanne. I make an effort to say yes to whatever I possibly can. Come on inside first. I have got to set this bag down."

Miss Pinkham unlocked the classroom door, and they went in.

"Now, what is it?"

"Well, I wondered if my rabbit, Hop, could come visit. I had to leave him behind on the island because no pets are allowed at my grandmother's apartment. But he's very good. He's no trouble at all. Well, once he did eat the lamp cord."

Miss Pinkham laughed.

"Of course he's welcome here. I'm glad you asked. Does he have a cage?"

"My dad made him one."

"Then he's welcome to join our other animals."

Rayanne leaped in the air with excitement.

Miss Pinkham opened her bag and began to unload her plan book and papers. On top was a flyer with a picture of a loon. She handed it to Rayanne.

"Hey," said Rayanne. "My gram just told me a story about a loon and its nest."

"That's interesting. Do you know a lot of traditional legends?"

Rayanne wrinkled her nose.

"I'm supposed to, but sometimes I forget. My grandmother tells great stories, though."

"Well, this poster's about the Maine Loon Project. They're looking for some students to help mark loon nesting sites this Friday. Would you be interested in being our fourth-grade volunteer? You'd have to do some canoeing, it says here."

"Sure, if my mom says I can. I'm a pretty good canoer."

Rayanne studied the flyer carefully.

"You know," said Miss Pinkham, "I've seen you look longingly out the window during class. This project is cold, hard work, but you get to miss a day of school to do it."

"I'm sure my mom will say yes," Rayanne said quickly. A day outdoors!

"Great!" laughed Miss Pinkham. "Now, scram. I've only got ten minutes to get my life in order before the first bell. Bring Hop in whenever you want."

Rayanne ran happily down the stairs and out onto the playground. She folded up the flyer on loons and put it in her pocket for later. When she shoved her hand in her pocket, she suddenly realized there was no crayon of the week in there. She'd forgotten to choose one, and this was Monday morning. Oh well, she thought, she'd had a lot on her mind, making plans for Hop.

She ran over to the swings, where Katie and Crissy were rocking back and forth on the swing seats with their heels dug into the sand. Rayanne swung herself around on the support pole.

"Guess what?" she asked.

"What?" said Katie.

"Miss Pinkham said it would be okay if my rabbit came to school."

"Neat! Is he cute?" asked Katie.

"Yup." Rayanne swung once around the pole.

"Does he bite?" asked Crissy. "I had a rabbit that used to bite."

"Nope." She swung around again. "He's really friendly. He just has to sniff you first. Then everything's okay. And you know what else?"

Some other kids had gathered around, including Scott.

"I'm going to miss almost a whole day of school on Friday," announced Rayanne.

"Why?" asked Crissy.

"I know," said Katie. "I bet you have to go to the dentist."

"Nope. I'm going on a school project. I'm going canoeing."

"Canoeing is awesome," Scott said. "Hey, how come you get to go and we don't?"

Rayanne fought the urge to turn away from him. She forced herself to answer.

"Because," she said.

"Because why?" asked Scott.

The bell rang and they all started toward the door.

"Because Miss Pinkham asked me if I wanted to help mark loon nesting sites for the Loon Project, and I said yes."

"Yeah? Cool," Scott replied. He ran off to join his friends.

That night, Rayanne told her mother how Miss Pinkham had agreed to let Hop stay in the classroom with the other animals.

"Oh, Rayanne, that's wonderful," her mother said, giving her a hug.

"I just thought I'd ask her and she said yes." Rayanne danced around the kitchen.

"It never hurts to ask, I guess," Gram said.

"Oh, I almost forgot." Rayanne dug around in her book bag. "She also gave me this. It's a permission slip for me to go on a canoe trip to help mark loon nesting sites."

Her mother took the notice and looked it over.

"It says here, Ray, to dress warmly and be ready to do a lot of paddling. Bring a lunch. Are you sure you want to go?"

"Yes!" shouted Rayanne. She was twirling in circles again.

"Are there other kids going?" her mom asked.

"Not from my class. I'm the fourth-grade volunteer. Just me."

Gram laughed. "So, you're the big adventurer!"

Rayanne flashed her a grin.

"If your teacher says it's okay, I guess it's all right. But you wear a life jacket the whole time, do you hear me?" her mother said.

"Yes," said Rayanne, nodding.

She couldn't wait for Friday. The next three days seemed endless. Every day after school, she pestered Gram for chores to do to make the time go faster. All Thursday afternoon, she helped Gram at the Xerox machine. The humming noise was so loud that she didn't hear Zak come up behind her.

"Boo!"

Rayanne jumped. She whirled around and saw Zak and Gram smiling at her.

"Hey, you scared me!" she said.

"Good," he said, grinning. "So, are you guys coming to the play? It's next week."

"Of course we are," Gram replied, collecting a pile of papers from the tray.

"Zak, guess what," Rayanne said. "I get to miss a whole day of school Friday. I'm going canoeing."

Zak nodded appreciatively. "Most excellent."

Gram loaded the cassette with fresh paper and started the machine up again.

"Hey, am I in your way or anything?" Zak asked, pretending to lie flat on the machine.

"Not if you stand over by the office counter where you belong," Gram answered.

Zak gave a big sigh. "I was just leaving anyway. See you, Rayanne. Say hi to the Wilburforce for me!"

And he ducked out of the office.

"Gram, do you think it will rain tomorrow?" Rayanne asked fretfully.

"Of course not. It's going to be a beautiful day. It says so right in the newspaper. It's over on the counter. Go take a look, while I finish up."

Rayanne opened the paper to the weather page

and crawled under the lost-and-found table to study it. A picture of a smiling sun stared back at her.

Sure enough, when Friday came, it was warm and sunny. Rayanne waited in the entryway by the school office dressed in jeans and a sweatshirt, holding her jacket and bag lunch. The last bell had rung and classes had already started when she saw a dark green van pull up in front of the school. An aluminum canoe was strapped to the van's roof. A young woman dressed in a down vest, plaid shirt, and hiking shorts jumped out and hurried up the sidewalk. Rayanne opened the door and let her in.

"Hi," the young woman said, "I'm Julie. Are you Rayanne?"

She put out her hand, and Rayanne shook it, a little self-conscious.

"Ready to go? I'll let the office know we're all set," Julie said. "You can head on out if you want."

Rayanne went down the sidewalk and climbed into the high front seat of the van, fumbling with the clasp on the unfamiliar seat belt. Julie followed a moment later. She climbed in on the driver's side and started the engine.

Soon they were on the highway. It was nearly an hour's drive north to Umbagog Pond. The October maples were brilliant with red and yellow leaves. In between the maples, the pine green evergreens stood silent and unchanging. This week's color is pine green, Rayanne decided, but she still hadn't remembered to pick out a crayon. She'd been too busy.

She was so glad to be out of school that she didn't mind the long ride. The lake they were going to post had a public beach at one end and lots of marshy, reedy areas for loons to nest in. It also had a low, reedy island in the center, just like in Gram's story.

"Here we are," said Julie. "You can see this lake has a lot of good loon sites. A couple of pairs already live here. But then there's the beach. If people come too close to the sites, the loons will leave and not come back. So I guess we have a lot of work to do."

She smiled encouragingly at Rayanne.

"Here comes the hard part."

Rayanne watched while Julie got ready to lower the canoe from the roof of the van. It was long and awkward. She untied it, then pushed it until it hung out way over the back of the van. She stood underneath it, holding the two seat struts over her head.

"Watch out, Rayanne," Julie called.

Julie gave a big heave. The back end of the canoe dropped in the sand. She lowered the canoe quickly and then tipped it right side up. Then Julie picked up the front, and Rayanne lifted the back a little, and they carried it in short bursts to the water's edge. Rayanne strapped on her life jacket while Julie loaded the nesting site signs into the canoe. For a moment, they looked at each other, sizing each other up. Then they pushed off.

It was a clear, breezy day. The sunlight glinted on the waves like bouncing stars. Rayanne took her paddle and dug in deep. She loved canoeing. In no time, they'd nearly reached the island.

"Wow," said Julie. "You're a really good paddler."

"My dad taught me," Rayanne said, turning around on her wicker seat.

"I guess he did. To tell the truth, I'd been expecting an older student, so when we first got here, I was wondering if you'd be able to handle the canoe," Julie admitted.

Rayanne smiled.

"I wondered the same about you."

Julie laughed.

"I guess we were both pretty suspicious. But we're doing all right now. I think we'll get this whole pond posted today."

Julie found a shallow spot and pounded the first nesting sign in. All morning, they paddled to different spots along the shore, pounding in signs. For lunch, they paddled to the middle of the lake and drifted, rocking to and fro on the small waves while they ate their sandwiches.

Suddenly, Julie pointed to a reedy area on the island, not far from them. A loon had just entered the water, paddling along, his sleek black head looking about. Rayanne could see his red-circled eye and his speckled necklace.

He tipped back his head and let out his wild, hooting cry. *Hoo hooo.* Rayanne shivered at the sound as it echoed across the lake. Nothing else in the world sounds like that, she thought. Cool and echoey and odd. It makes me feel complete, and that's the shivery part. The loon's hooting call reminded her of Gram's story. She remembered that the loon was Koluskap's messenger, bringing them news of something important, something wild that's always here. She wondered if Julie felt like that, too. She turned around.

Julie smiled.

"There's nothing like it, is there?" she asked.

Rayanne shook her head and together they watched the loon dive deep into the lake.

Chapter 11
Starlight

THAT NIGHT, Rayanne sat wedged in Gram's arm-chair, studying her books. She read all the parts about Merlin in the King Arthur book several times. He was a little bit like Gram, she thought, although he had wispy, white hair and crinkled cheeks and Gram didn't, and he seemed to know about things before they happened. Nothing took him by surprise, like when young King Arthur appeared in the woods, Merlin already knew who he was even though he'd never seen him before. Rayanne liked the part about seeing into the future. She also liked his purple robe.

She could easily do her next book project for Miss Pinkham now. It had to be a poster showing an important scene from a book you'd just read. Miss Pinkham would be so surprised when Rayanne walked in with a poster of King Arthur pulling the sword out of the stone. Or should she draw a moose ducking his head for pondweed? Either way, it was a big change from *Everett, the Runaway Donkey.* Rayanne laughed, thinking of the surprised look on Miss Pinkham's face. Miss Pinkham was pretty nice. It would be fun to surprise her with a really great project.

"I need lots of black paper and something glittery for stars," announced Rayanne at breakfast the next morning. "I have to do a big book project for Open House. It's got to be good."

It was Saturday, and Gram was making waffles. They had all agreed that they needed a change from cold cereal.

Rayanne spooned the thick, gooey batter into the waffle iron and lowered the lid. Batter oozed out around the edges and began to puff up in satisfying bulges.

"Hmm," said her mother. "I can't think what we have that's glittery."

"I have a scrap box someplace," Gram said.

"With buttons, sequins, and cloth. I don't know if that's what you had in mind."

"Great!" said Rayanne, laying down the spoon with the waffle batter on it. "Where is it?"

"One thing at a time," laughed Gram. "I'll look for it after breakfast."

"So, how are things going at school, Ray?" Mom asked.

"Oh, better. I just read a really great book on King Arthur. And one on Maine animals. Wait until Miss Pinkham sees my book project."

Gram opened the waffle iron and carefully worked the waffle loose. She put the sections of waffle on plates and passed them to Rayanne and her mother.

"These are great!" said Ray, pouring a hefty dose of syrup on top of hers. "I wish we could do a play like Zak does at the high school. But Miss Pinkham is pretty exciting. We have a lizard, at least. I can't wait till we go visit Ann Marie next week, so we can get Hop."

"Are you sure Miss Pinkham said it was okay, keeping all those animals in her classroom?" asked her mother.

"Sure," Rayanne replied. "She has a telescope we can borrow sometime, too. Gram, is there a way we could get up on the roof of this building?"

"I've never been up there," Gram said. "But I'm sure we could find out."

Rayanne ate a couple of pieces of waffle.

"I like waffles much better than cold cereal. Thanks, Gram."

"You're welcome, dear."

Ray laughed, thinking of antlers.

When they finished eating, her mother said, "We'll clean up the kitchen so Gram can go look for the scrap box, okay, Ray?"

"Okay, dear," said Rayanne. Gram winked at her.

Rayanne and her mother wiped up the spilled blobs of waffle batter, sponged off the table, and washed the dishes.

Meanwhile, Gram had found the box and some scissors. Now she was hunting for glue.

There was a knock at the door.

"I'll get it," shouted Rayanne, running to open it.

She turned the bolt and slid the chain off. The door opened. There was her father.

Rayanne gasped and stepped backward. She grabbed ahold of the edge of the door, as if to slam it shut.

"Hello, Ray. Can I come in?" her father asked.

"Ray, who is it?"

Her mother came down the hall. Rayanne turned and walked deliberately and calmly down the hall to her bed in the living room. She picked up the King Arthur book and climbed onto the bed with it.

This wasn't happening the right way, she thought. Where were the horses and the tall prairie grass? Where were the blizzards and mountain trails and secret army spy equipment?

Now here was her father, at the door, looking small and ordinary. Not brave or noble, just regular, like cold cereal or an old sweatshirt on the lost-and-found table. He was just a person who couldn't be trusted, that was all.

Why would Mom even talk to him? Why did she let him in? She should banish him, send him back out to the sidewalks and gas stations and stoplights, all those everyday places where nothing special ever happened.

King Arthur would have given him a punishment. He would have made her dad fight a fire-breathing dragon or a wild wolverine, the most evil of the forest animals, before he would be allowed to come back. Maybe Koluskap would have squeezed him into a bullfrog and made him sit in mud. Someone should have to decide what the punishment should be. That was only fair.

"Ray," called her mother. "Can you come out here?"

"No," yelled Rayanne. "Tell him to go away."

Then she thought, what if he did go away again? Would that really be better?

She slipped off the daybed and started down the hall.

Her father sat at the kitchen table. Her mother had poured him a cup of coffee. Gram was nowhere to be seen. Her purse was not on the little table by the telephone where it usually was.

"Where's Gram?" asked Ray, not looking at her father.

"She went out for a few minutes. She'll be right back," said her mother.

"I better go find her," Rayanne said tensely, grabbing her jacket from the hook by the door.

"Ray." Her mother grabbed her shoulders. "It's all right. Gram's not going to leave. Come on."

Her mother sat her at the table. Rayanne swung her foot slowly back and forth and stared at the floor. Her body was so still, she hardly felt her own breathing. She felt pure and clean in her rage. That would be the punishment, then. No dragons or wolverines. She would show her father how angry she was. She wouldn't flinch or soften the blow.

"I'm sorry you're so mad at me," her father said.

Rayanne didn't answer. It wasn't fair that if she didn't do her homework, she got punished, but if he didn't do what he was supposed to do, nothing happened at all.

"It's not fair," she said. Hot, angry tears filled her eyes.

"I agree," said her mother.

"How about we take a ride up to Bangor and look at the shops?" her father suggested.

"No," said Rayanne. "I don't want to."

There was a silence. Rayanne heard her sulky, stubborn voice linger on in her own ears. Good, she thought. I'm glad I sound that way.

"Did you use those crayons I gave you for your birthday?" he asked.

Rayanne nodded.

"Where did you go?" she asked. "In the red car."

"Well, Ray, sometimes you feel that you just need a chance to start over. That the first time you did something, you hardly knew what you were doing. Can you understand that?"

Rayanne felt confused.

"You mean when you had me, you didn't know what you were doing?" she asked.

"No, no. Nothing like that."

"Well, then, what?" shouted Rayanne. "Somebody tell me!"

"I'm getting remarried soon, Ray. I went away for a while to think it over, to make sure that's what I want to do. And I'm going to move south, to Portland, and get trained as a finish carpenter."

Rayanne looked at her mother. She had her tired look again.

"I'm sorry, Ray," her mom said. "I thought maybe we could just wait it out, maybe go back to the way things were before. I guess I was wrong."

Ray's head ached, but she felt less tense. She sighed.

"Did you go to Montana or not?" she asked.

"I was there for about a week. That red car? It broke down out there. I had to take the bus back."

Rayanne thought that over.

"Listen, Ray. I shouldn't have burst in like this, but I didn't know how else to do it. I have a telephone now. I'll leave the phone number with you, okay? I won't be moving to Portland for another month or two. All right?"

All right? thought Ray. Why does he keep asking that?

Rayanne nodded, but she didn't look as he wrote down the number on a slip of paper. Her mom reached out and took it.

"Do you miss the island?" Ray asked.

He gave a short laugh.

"Of course I do. But I decided I had to move on for a while, like a migrating bird, I guess."

Rayanne turned her head away, remembering how the redwing blackbirds left the island in the winter, but they always came back.

Rayanne lay on her bed, staring at the wall, thinking. So it all turned out to be nothing mysterious. Her father was marrying someone else, that was all. Rayanne knew that had happened to other kids, like Zak. They got stepmothers and step-fathers.

Why had she never thought of it? Why had she thought of so many other things— spies, prairies, cowboys, knights, blizzards?

She flipped over on her back and stared at the ceiling. You could tell yourself great stories about castles and spies and loons and blizzards, like Gram did. Exciting stories that could go on and on, comforting you, and you could change them around whenever you wanted to. No one could tell you how it was going to turn out, and Rayanne liked that part. That's why she liked to look at picture books and make up her own stories.

But what kind of story could you make up about your dad leaving one day and then marrying someone else? Where were the good guys and the bad guys, and the terrible adventures that had to be overcome? In this story, it was all mixed up. Her mom was good, but she was so busy working, and she had sort of been just like Rayanne, hoping things would sooner or later go back to the way they were before.

People were good and bad at the same time, all mixed up together, and they just had to keep trying to do better. Big deal, she thought.

Gram came into the living room. She walked over to Ray's bed. Rayanne turned toward the wall.

"Ray, dear, when I went out this morning, I went to the mall and got some sequins, and I looked for stars, too. I even got you some glow-in-the-dark puff paint so you could make some stars yourself."

Ray turned toward Gram. Gram sat on the edge of the bed, holding the black paper and the scrap box.

"I think things are going to work out, Ray. It's better that you see your dad a little and that he hasn't completely disappeared," Gram said in a matter-of-fact voice. "Soon it won't be so hard."

"He's sort of half vanished?" asked Ray.

"That's usually the way things go," said Gram. "Not much ends up all neat and tidy. Now, let's take a look at this puff paint. It's yellow and it glows in the dark. Won't that be exciting? Or how about this glitter? I thought maybe some stars and half-moons might look good. What do you think?"

Rayanne sat up on her knees. Her dad would have to wait awhile. Right now, she wanted to plan out her book project with Gram. She could almost hear Zak's voice, urging her to *do* something, not to be a fungus. Zak was funny.

She looked at the glitter and a pack of glow-in-the-dark star stickers. Gram had found some really great things. She picked up the scissors and a piece of the black paper.

"I think I'll cut some loon shapes out and try out some of the different glitter and stars first. Maybe I'll call Dad later, when I get my project figured out. But I can't see him next weekend because we're going up to the island to pick up Hop and visit Ann Marie. I haven't seen Ann Marie for two whole months!"

"I know," said Gram.

"Ann Marie said she really, really misses me, especially because Adam and Jason are still in her class. They are the worst, Gram. Really. Her mother said maybe I could visit with them on the island this summer while you and Mom are working. Hey, Gram, do you think that if we called Julie, I could go out and post another pond sometime? You know, those people on the beach should learn to leave those loons alone. Maybe I should be a park ranger when I grow up."

Gram smiled. "Maybe," she said. "You're full of surprises."

"Right," agreed Rayanne.

Then, concentrating, she cut out the loon, its wings outspread. She swooped it in the air and then made it dive deep under the water. There the loon swam swiftly, darting through the weeds, surprising the fish. She remembered his wild, hooting call and the scattered white speckles on his back. Gram's stories helped her remember.

Penobscot meant the rocky place. While the river hurried past, the rocks stayed, hard and steadfast. Rayanne was going to keep her promise and go back for Hop. In her imagination, she saw herself with Gram and Mom, crossing the Two Rivers bridge to the island, on their way to Ann Marie's. Ray smiled. Hadn't she told Hop she wouldn't forget? She was a rock in the river, a star in the sky.

Author's Note

The double-curve designs that appear at the end of each chapter are very meaningful to the Wabanaki people, including the Penobscot. Along with geometric and floral designs and pictures of animals, double-curve designs were painted and embroidered on clothing, canoes, wigwams, and many other items.

The Penobscot designs in *Crossing the Starlight Bridge* were originally collected and published in 1914 by Frank G. Speck, an anthropologist who studied the Northeast Algonquin tribes. They are reproduced in *The Wabanakis of Maine and the Maritimes: A Resource Book About the Penobscot,*

Passamaquoddy, Maliseet, Micmac, and Abenaki Indians, prepared for and published by the Maine Indian Program of the New England Regional Office of the American Friends Service Committee in 1989. In this important resource, it is explained that "the spiral, which is basic to the double-curve design, still has a special meaning among the Wabanaki people. It is a pattern found often in nature, whether in the coil of the fiddlehead fern or the paths animals take when bedding down so that any animal following must, while following the spiral path, come upwind of them."

I wish to express my thankfulness to the many teachers, writers, and historians who worked for five years preparing *The Wabanakis of Maine and the Maritimes.* It is an inspiring book. I have read it many times and know I will read it many more.